William G. McLeod

The Dunvegan and the Montrose

William G. McLeod

The Dunvegan and the Montrose

ISBN/EAN: 9783337417369

Printed in Europe, USA, Canada, Australia, Japan

Cover: Foto ©Andreas Hilbeck / pixelio.de

More available books at **www.hansebooks.com**

The DUNVEGAN & the MONTROSE

BEING A DESCRIPTION *of the* APARTMENT HOTELS *just erected on the corner of* MASSACHUSETTS AVE. & SHEPARD ST.. CAMBRIDGE *with Sundry Pictures and Plans*

CAMBRIDGE · PRINTED FOR THE OWNER BY WILL BRADLEY AT THE UNIVERSITY PRESS · 1899

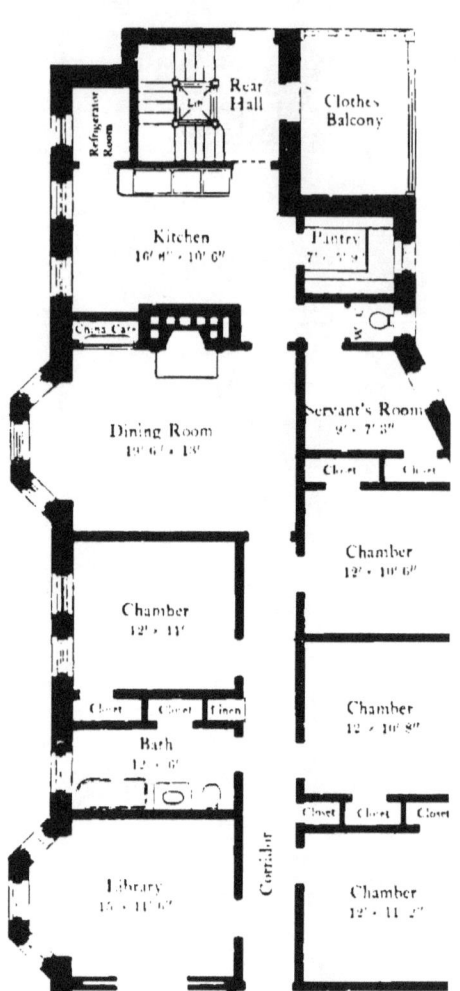

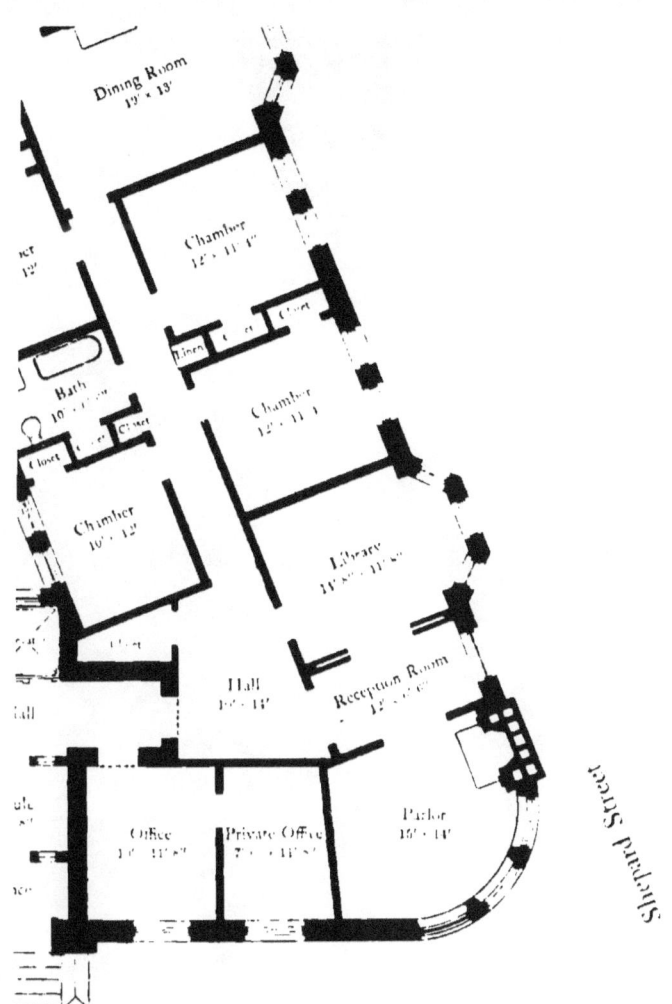

Dining Room
19' × 13'

Chamber
14' × 11' 4"

Chamber
12'

Chamber
12' × 11'

Bath
10' × 9'

Linen   Closet   Closet

Closet

Chamber
10' × 12'

Closet   Closet

Closet

Library
13' × 11' 6"

Closet

Hall
15' × 14'

Reception Room
12' × 7' 6"

Parlor
15' × 14'

Office
14' × 11' 6"

Private Office
7' × 11' 6"

Shepard Street

Massachusetts Avenue

FOREWORD

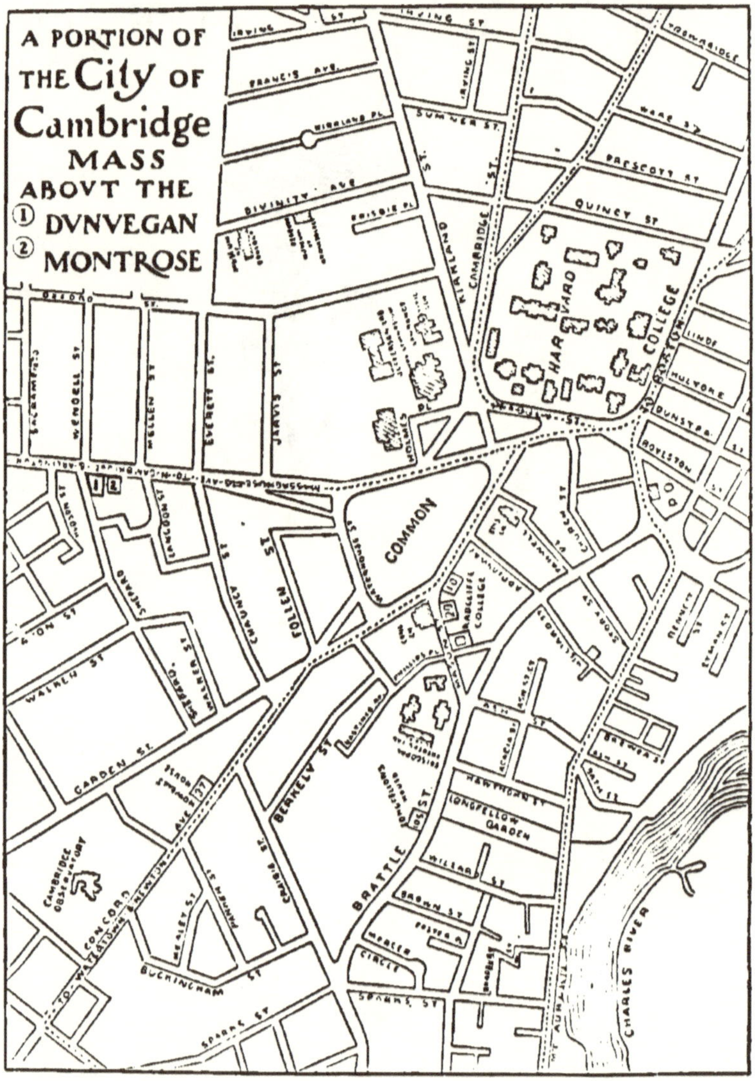

A PORTION OF
THE City OF
Cambridge
MASS
ABOVT THE
① DVNVEGAN
② MONTROSE

*Diagram
showing
Location
of the
1 Dunvegan
&
2 Montrose*

FOREWORD

HE object of this little book is to introduce the new Cambridge apartment hotels, the *Dunvegan* and the *Montrose*, which offer to prospective tenants a combination of advantages unequalled in Cambridge, and considering their moderate rental, unsurpassed in Boston or the surburban districts.

The Dunvegan and Montrose

Cambridge has many attractions as a place of residence. Among these are its splendid historic and literary traditions; its exceptional educational advantages by reason of its fine public and private schools and as the seat of Harvard University and Radcliffe College; its fine residences, churches, clubs, parks, and public drives; its proximity and easy access to Boston; and the moral standing, general intelligence, and refinement of its people.

Residential Attractions of Cambridge

F O R E W O R D

Location  The Dunvegan and the Montrose,
standing as they do at the corner of
Massachusetts Avenue and Shepard Street,
have a location that is unsurpassed in the
city. The electric cars, which run every
two or three minutes, stop at the door.
The trip to Bowdoin Square or to Park
Street Station is made in about thirty
minutes, or by steam cars from Porter
Station in about fifteen minutes. The
location is also just at the meeting-place
of the finest old residential section and the
finest new. In the immediate neighbor-
hood are the streets, houses, and historic
spots made famous by their associations
with the great men and the great events
of the past. Two blocks distant is the
old Cambridge Common, "the first camp-
ground of the Revolution," on one side
of which stands Radcliffe College and on
the other Harvard University. By this
proximity an opportunity is given of at-
tending the public lectures, readings, and
concerts given under the auspices of the
University, and of seeing and hearing the
many noted visitors to the University
both from this country and from abroad.

DUNVEGAN

The DUNVEGAN

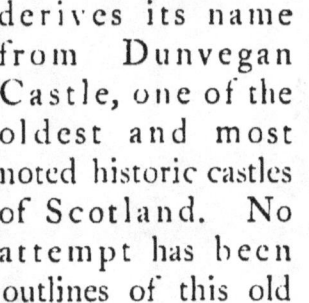

HE DUNVEGAN *Name* derives its name from Dunvegan Castle, one of the oldest and most noted historic castles of Scotland. No attempt has been made to follow the outlines of this old feudal castle, but the same feeling of strength, solidity, and massive dignity has in a large measure been reproduced. The coat of arms of the castle has been introduced into the stained glass windows, and its mottoes "Hold fast" and "Murus aheneus esto" (Stand like a bulwark) may fitly stand as the keynote of the building's construction.

The building is six stories in height, with a frontage of eighty-five feet on Massachusetts Avenue. The foundation is of granite, and the walls of the best light gray mottled bricks and Indiana limestone; the timbers are supported by iron pillars; the framework is as stanch and strong as it was

Size and Materials possible to make it; and only the best seasoned and most carefully selected woods were used, so as to avoid the possibility of sagging, shrinkage, or vibration.

Light, Air, and View From the accompanying floor plans prepared by the architect, Mr. Willard M. Bacon, it will be seen that, with the exception of a common entrance, each half of the hotel is virtually a building by itself, and every room an outside room, admitting abundance of light and air. The windows of the upper stories afford a view in all directions that for extent and beauty can scarcely be surpassed.

The outer and inner vestibule are finished throughout in Siena marble, with mosaic floors, and with massive carved mahogany doors and casings, surrounded at the top and on either side by stained glass windows. The hall on the first floor has a dado of Siena marble, which extends up the stairway to the floor above. The doors and casings are of mahogany, and the floors of mosaic. The front stairway from the first to the second story is of mahogany, with marble treads. All other stairs, hall floors, doors, and casings are of quartered oak. The halls are abundantly lighted by double windows of leaded glass on each floor, opening into the central court.

Halls and Stairs

Decorations The wall decorations are from original designs specially prepared for this building by Mr. Will Bradley, and put on under his supervision.

Elevator The building is furnished with an automatic electric elevator, which is provided with appliances for convenience and safety that represent the highest reach hitherto attained in elevator construction. The cage and grill-work being of antique bronze, make a handsome appearance. This elevator is in charge of a competent person at all times.

Besides the electric bells and speaking-tubes in the vestibule for each suite, there is an annunciator in charge of the janitor, with speaking-tubes that connect with each suite and enable every tenant to call and converse with the janitor.

The building is thoroughly wired for electric lights, and piped for gas, and furnished with handsome gas and electric fixtures. *Bells, Tubes, and Lighting*

The heating is what is known as the low-pressure, hot-water system. With two hot-water boilers of over ten thousand feet capacity it is possible to bid defiance to the coldest winter. Radiators are placed in all rooms, and an equable temperature is maintained through the entire building. There is also a separate plant which furnishes all kitchens and bathrooms with an abundant supply of hot water at all hours and at all seasons of the year. *Heating*

Basements The basement contains the janitor's apartments, bicycle room, and rooms for the storage of trunks and furniture.

Number and The building contains twelve family *Size of* suites of ten rooms and bath, and twelve *Suites* bachelor suites of two rooms and bath. The large suites consist of parlor, reception-room, library, dining-room, four chambers, kitchen and servant's chamber, bath-room, servant's water-closet, and butler's pantry. The rooms are of ample size and convenient arrangement. With suites of this size the conveniences of an apartment hotel are put within the reach

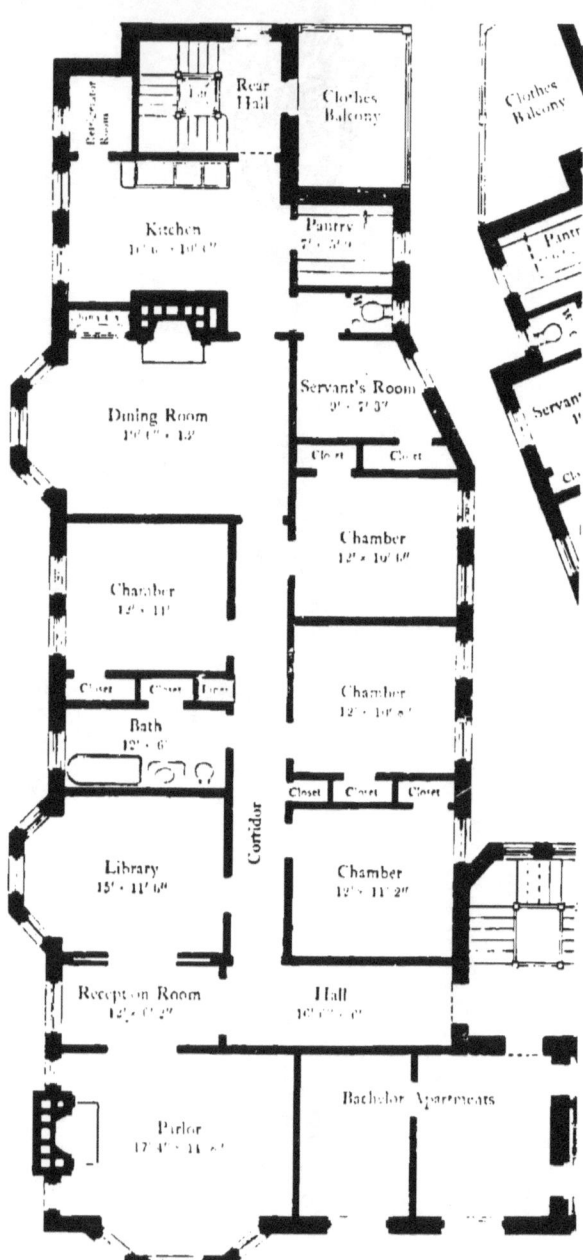

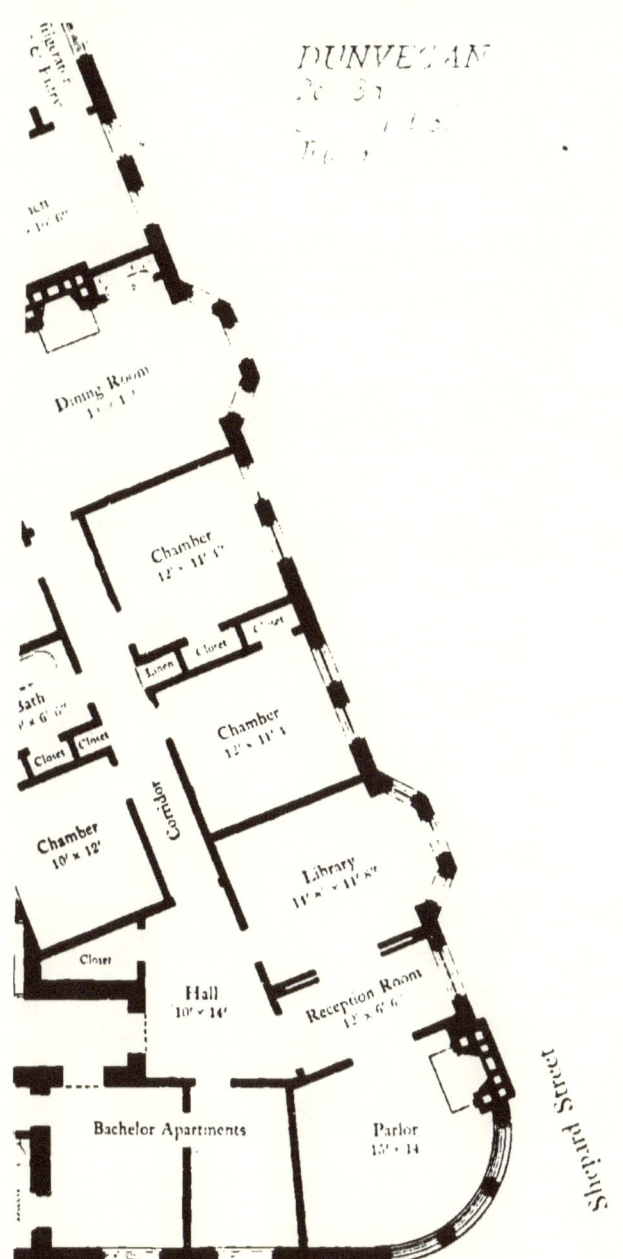

DUNVE.AN

Dining Room

Chamber
12' x 11' 5"

Linen Closet

Bath

Closet Closet

Chamber
12' x 11' 4

Chamber
10' x 12'

Corridor

Closet

Library
11' x 11' 8"

Hall
10' x 14'

Reception Room
12' x 6' 6"

Bachelor Apartments

Parlor
15' x 14

Shepard Street

Massachusetts Avenue

of people who desire the spacious accom-
modations that are ordinarily found only
in a private house.

The kitchen and butler's pantry are *Kitchen*
finished in cypress and ash, with hard- *and Pantry*
wood floors, and equipped with sink, set
tubs, and a gas range. The kitchen, like
the other rooms, is heated by a radiator,
and furnished with hot water from the
basement plant. A small room opens
from the kitchen which is designed for
a refrigerator and other uses which will
suggest themselves to the practical house-
keeper. The back stairway is provided
with a lift, and each suite has a back

Kitchen and Pantry piazza with hooks for drying clothes. The servant's chamber and water-closet being entered from the kitchen are thus kept distinct from the rest of the suite. The butler's pantry has abundant shelf and drawer room, and cupboards provided with patent barrel-swings.

Dining-Room The dining-room, in keeping with its importance in the domestic economy, is the largest and in some ways the most attractive room in the suite. It is finished in quartered oak, with a handsome panelled dado rubbed down to a dull finish. The floor is of oak, and is provided with an electric foot-button communicating with the kitchen. The room has a china closet, with drawers, shelves, and sliding doors of leaded glass. It has also a brick mantel and an open fireplace, which may be used either for wood or a gas log.

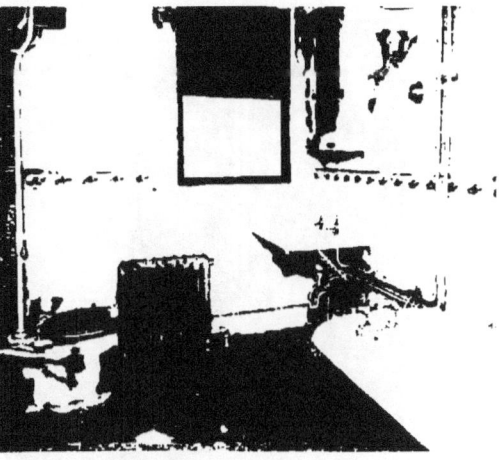

The other rooms are finished in white with a hard-pine *Other* floor in the corridor and oak floors in the *Rooms* entrance-hall, parlor, library, and reception-room. The parlor has an open fireplace, with a mantel and ornamental tiling. Care has been taken to lay out the rooms so as to permit of a proper disposition of the furniture and the best utilization of wall space.

A special feature of the building is the *Bath Rooms* large bath-rooms, with dados of solid tiling, mosaic floors, porcelain bath-tubs, bowls of Italian marble, medicine closets with adjustable shelves, and bevelled French plate mirrors, the best water-closets obtainable, and the finest open nickelled plumbing. Like all other rooms in the building they are outside rooms, and in

size and appearance as well as in sanitary qualities they are up to the very highest standard.

Closets Closet room, which is such an important practical feature in every apartment, has been generously provided. Besides a closet in each of the five chambers, there is a closet off the bath-room, a coat closet, and a linen closet opening from the corridor, and a very large closet off the entrance-hall. All closets are provided with shelves and hooks.

Windows The chambers have two windows, and all parlors, libraries, and dining-rooms have large bay windows commanding a view of the avenue. Most of the windows are

over five feet in width, and each sash con- *Windows*
tains a single light of heavy French plate,
bent glass being used in the bays. All
windows are furnished with linen curtains
of a uniform specially selected tint.

Perhaps no other item outside the fur- *Wall*
nishing of a room does so much to deter- *Papers*
mine its character and render it attractive
as the proper selection of wall papers.
The cost of the papers in this building
and the painstaking care devoted to their

Wall Papers

selection greatly exceeds the ordinary standard for such work. The papers show the newest and most artistic designs and colorings — many of them exclusive — in satin-finished papers, hand prints, aniline dyes, silk ingrains, French tapestries, and other choice domestic and imported goods. No two papers in the building are alike, and care has been taken to preserve a proper color-scheme for adjoining rooms and a unity of motive throughout each suite.

Bachelor Suites Besides the twelve family suites there are twelve bachelor suites of two rooms and a bath. These rooms are all in the front of the building overlooking Massachusetts Avenue, and are finished in white with an adamant dado and hard-wood floors. The bath-room is in every detail finished in the same handsome manner as the bath-room in the larger suites. Each suite has a large closet, and is provided with a separate gas and electric light meter, and with bells and-speaking tubes connecting with the vestibule and with the janitor's apartments.

Telephone There is also a long-distance telephone for the free use of the tenants in the building.

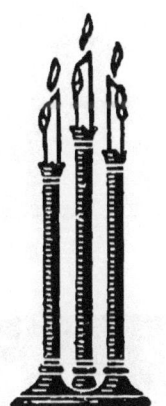

The MONTROSE

HE MONTROSE adjoins the Dunvegan on Massachusetts Avenue, and is a companion building to it. The buildings are twenty-five feet apart, and connected by a subway. They are of the same height, of about the same size, are built of the same materials, and while differing in detail, have the same general architectural appearance. The vestibules and first-story hall and stairway of the

Interior Montrose are finished in Siena marble and
mahogany with mosaic floors, and all other
halls and stairs in quartered oak in the same
manner as the Dunvegan. The elevator
and hot-water heating are of similar construction ; the plumbing is the same ; the
bath-rooms are similarly finished in solid
tiling and mosaic, and equipped with the
same bowls, closets, and bath-tubs, and
with a constant supply of hot water; the
wood-work, mantels, windows, closets,
hard-wood floors, painting, papering,
lighting, electric bells, and speaking-tubes,
and in general all the details of interior

construction, are the work of the same contractors and are of the same standard of excellence as in the Dunvegan.

The Montrose differs from the Dunve- *Minor* gan mainly in having no bachelor suites. *Differences* Each of its twelve suites consists of ten rooms and a bath of about the same size and substantially the same arrangement as in the Dunvegan. In the Montrose, however, one chamber opens into an interior light-well; and the parlor and library, instead of being separated by the reception-room, open directly into each other, and both face upon the avenue. The

suites on the south side of this building are particularly desirable on account of their sunny exposure and attractive out-look.

In the Montrose as in the Dunvegan, while no expense has been spared in the interests of thoroughness and perfection, the aim

Motive of both Buildings has been to present an appearance of richness and refinement such as a man of wealth and culture would desire to have in his private house but which is not ordinarily seen in a building of this nature.

Open Inspection All persons, whether prospective tenants or not, are cordially invited to come and be shown through these buildings, which must be seen to be properly appreciated.

Prices The moderate prices for which it has been found possible to rent these suites ought to prove not their least attractive feature. Terms and further particulars may be had from the janitor on the premises or by addressing the owner, William

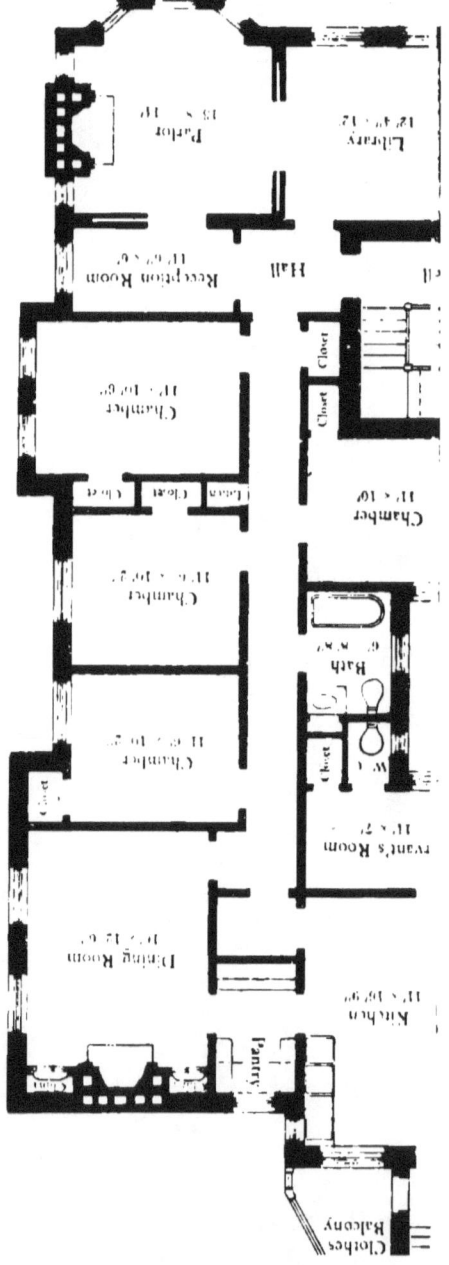

Massachusetts Avenue

Parlor
15' × 19'

Library
18' 4" × 19'

Reception Room
11' 6" × 9'

Hall

Chamber
11' × 10' 6"

Closet Closet

Closet Bath Closet

Chamber
11' × 10'

Chamber
11' 6" × 10' 2"

Bath
6' × 8'

Chamber
11' × 10' 3"

Closet W.C.

Servant's Room
11' × 7'

Dining Room
17' × 15' 6"

Kitchen
11' × 16' 9"

Pantry

Clothes
Balcony

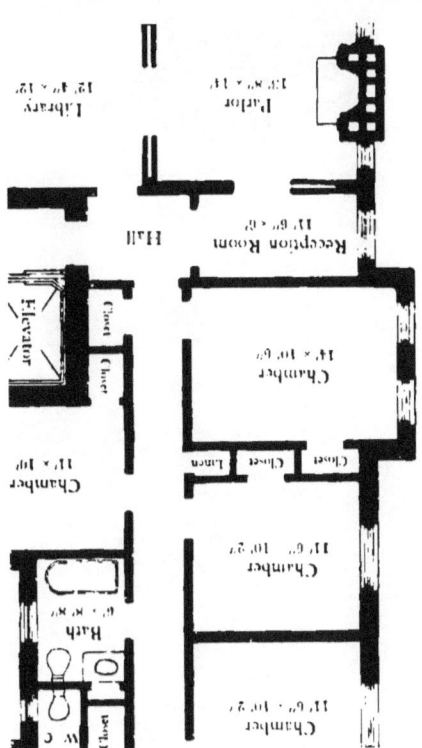

G. MacLeod, The Dunvegan, Cambridge
from whom copies of this book may be had
for the asking.